SOCCER HOUR

BY
CAROL NEVIUS

ILLUSTRATED BY
BILL THOMSON

MARSHALL CAVENDISH CHILDREN

To my sister, Pat Nevius, and all
youth soccer coaches   —C.N.

With love and appreciation to my wonderful in-laws,
Beatrice and Richard McDevitt   —B.T.

Bill Thomson embraced traditional painting techniques and meticulously painted each illustration by hand, using acrylic paint and colored pencils. Each illustration took about 100 hours to finish; his illustrations are not photographs or computer generated images.

Text copyright © 2011 by Carol Nevius
Illustrations copyright © 2011 by Bill Thomson
All rights reserved
Marshall Cavendish Corporation, 99 White Plains Road,
Tarrytown, NY 10591
www.marshallcavendish.us/kids
Library of Congress Cataloging-in-Publication Data
Nevius, Carol, 1955-
Soccer hour / by Carol Nevius ;
illustrated by Bill Thomson. — 1st ed.
p. cm. Summary: Pictures and rhyming text
describe the drills and scrimmages of a team at
soccer practice. ISBN 978-0-7614-5689-6
[1. Stories in rhyme. 2. Soccer—Fiction.]
I. Thomson, Bill, 1963- ill. II. Title.
PZ8.3.N374So 2010 [E]—dc22
2009014112
Book design by Michael Nelson
Editor: Margery Cuyler
Printed in China [E]
First edition
1 3 5 6 4 2

Marshall Cavendish
Children

SOCCER IS A GLOBAL GAME,
FÚTBOL IS ITS OTHER NAME,
A TEAM SPORT PLAYED WITH MOSTLY FEET
ON FIELDS AND LAWNS AND IN THE STREET.

IN SOCCER HOUR we learn to think;
we come prepared with ball and drink.
We practice playing as a team.
A winning season is our dream.

We stretch. Our coaches help us learn.

We warm up taking shots in turn.
We stop the ball, take careful aim,
kick toward the corner of the frame.

We toss the ball up in the air
and juggle it to keep it there.
We try to bounce a steady beat
with heads and thighs as well as feet.

We jump small hurdles, bending knees;
weave through cones in groups of threes.
Our trainer shows us footwork tricks—
fake-out moves and rainbow kicks.

Keep-away is a practice drill
of ball control, defensive skill.
"Keep possession of the ball,
pass and trap, one touch for all."

We scrimmage, split the team in two,
"Throw down the line, Red. Mark up, Blue!"

We listen for a teammate's call.
Dribble, pass . . . Red steals the ball.
Soon they take a shot on goal.
Blue team blocks, but can't control.

Our keeper charges, yells commands,
lunges, grabs the ball with hands.
We're running backward, spreading out.
I hear my name as the goalie shouts.

I meet the punt, then trap it down.
We work to keep it on the ground.

I see my teammate in the clear
and cross it as he's running near.

He heads it . . .

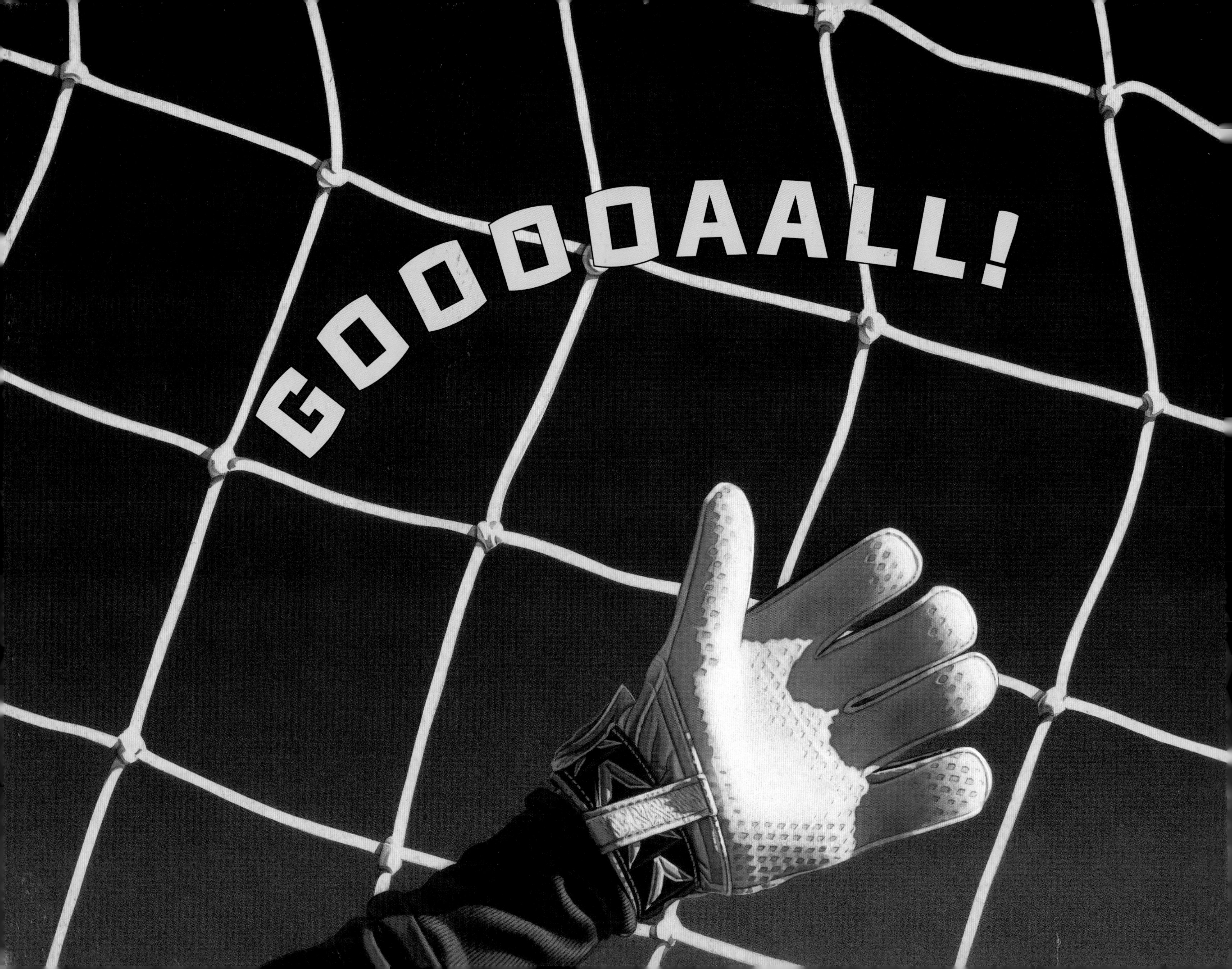
GOOOOAALL!

We clap and shout, "High fives! That's right!"
We're getting better every night.

When time is up and practice ends,
we jog together, tired friends.
This Soccer Hour of work and play
will help us win next Saturday!